One Hour: Total Surrender

Alexis Ryder

Published by Alexis Ryder, 2024.

ONE HOUR:
Total Surrender
Smashwords Edition
Alexis Ryder

This is a work of fiction. Similarities to real people, places, or events are entirely coincidental.

ONE HOUR: TOTAL SURRENDER

First edition. January 11, 2024.

Copyright © 2024 Alexis Ryder.

ISBN: 979-8227287397

Written by Alexis Ryder.

Also by Alexis Ryder

One Hour: Total Surrender

Table of Contents

CHAPTER 1

Friday night, exactly 9 pm, and nine days before Christmas; I'm sitting alone, a reputable attorney at Lawrence & Kofax, staring at the dark liquid in my glass. I look up to see that the bar is surprisingly empty; just me and the barman for now. Mirrors shine on the wall. The floor is meticulously clean. Polished wood tables sit empty, waiting for people to use them. The Gold Leaf Bar is the kind of establishment that's usually frequented by people that can afford ten dollars or more for a single drink.

Outside on the street, people are in a hurry. Traffic bustles. Taillights blend with Christmas lights that have been strung along the boulevard to infuse festiveness into the air. Pedestrians walk side by side, smiling and talking to one another. Some walk in a faster gait smiling while having a cell phone pressed against their ear. Every stranger I see I can sense their excitement for the holiday, I'm not at all feeling festive. Still, I lift my glass and raise it with my eyes on the nearest window. "Merry Christmas," I offer silently, because although I'm not feeling my best I'm glad to see others taking the time to enjoy a Friday night like it should be enjoyed.

'Telling yourself Merry Christmas as well might make you feel better.'

My eyes travel to the right of me where the voice comes from. I'm not only stunned to see someone sitting two stools from me, I'm questioning how I could have missed him before when minutes ago the bartender and I seemed to be alone. I look past the stranger to see if maybe he came from a door across the room, but the only thing I see is the small hall where the restrooms sit. I stare at him again because people just don't materialise out of thin air and I haven't finished my first glass of liquor to use the excuse of being drunk. Another reason I'm looking at him questionably is how he knew I wished strangers on the street a Merry Christmas. I didn't speak the words out loud. Hell, I barely raised my glass, but here he is, his brown eyes boring into me like he knows everything about me, including all of my secrets.

I smile on this thought and turn my gaze from him, lift my glass, raise it to my mouth, then watch as my hand trembles, the liquor threatens to spill, my heart races, my breathing increases, and I'm frightened to look at the stranger again because he's no longer sitting two seats over.

He's now directly beside me.

My eyes glance quickly to the side confirming he is close then turning back to the glass I raise it with a flourish, '*Well, here's to you Justine, happy end of relationship day and Merry Fucking Christmas too.*' I whisper before downing the contents in one gulp. The warm liquid momentarily causes me gasp hitting me like an express train with the shock, C— coughing, I placed the glass back on the bar with a resounding "thud."

'Another,' I order with a splutter. 'And, make it a double.' The bartender regards me for a moment with a look that speaks almost mockingly: "*this broad is a light weight when it comes to her liquor"* he shrugs then refills the glass. I sit quietly staring fascinated by the dark liquid as I once again swirl it around in the bottom of the glass.

'Whatever it is your searching for, you won't find it in there.' Comes the voice again.

Jolted back to reality I turn to face the figure sitting next to me. 'Excuse me?'

'I said, whatever it is you're looking for, you won't find it in there,' he replies indicating to the glass in my hand. For a moment words fail me on how to respond. Should I be angry at the interruption or grateful? He is perhaps late 30's to early 40's, with dark well groomed slick backed hair and the well cut navy suit give him the look of a fellow lawyer. He sits half turned towards me relaxed holding a drink in his right hand. Despite the cut of his suit it fails to hide the broad shoulders and thick set neck. His brown eyes smile with a deep alluring penetrating softness causing an involuntary ache in my nipples.

'Is that a double bourbon?' His question cuts my train of thought and sensations.

'Yeah.' I find myself admitting. Keeping myself from turning fully to face him and revealing the now tell tale arousal through my thin blouse.

'Then you are indeed in trouble. Looks like I arrived just in the nick of time.'

'Not that it's any of your business.' I reply sharply.

'No. You're absolutely right. Please.' He smiles holding up his hands in mock surrender. 'Don't shoot. I apologise for intruding, it really is none of my business. But, I can tell you from personal experience that, that...' He says pointing to the glass. 'Won't help resolve whatever issues you're trying to deal with.'

'And what, makes you think I have issues?' My tone is not friendly.

'Well, let's see, shall we?' Says the man sitting back slightly on his stool. 'One very attractive, well-dressed and clearly, successful woman, sitting alone, looking all forlorn in a bar on a Friday night, contemplating downing a double bourbon. Now tell me honestly — what's wrong with this picture?'

I allow myself a small smile. 'You're very perceptive.'

'Not really. Just gleaned from a lot of experience. And I have a confession. I've been where you are right now.'

I make to respond but he holds up a hand. 'I'd say right now you're trying to decide whether to take the plunge into getting blind drunk, in the hope it'll numb the pain within. You're sort of like the jumper about to leap off a cliff or a building.'

'I don't think I like your analogy,' I growl.

'That tells me I'm right then.' He replies.

'Almost' I hear myself admit then mentally kick myself hard. Who the hell is this guy?

'So why don't you tell me about it?'

I glance up at the man for a moment, feeling my blood begin boil at his continual presumptuousness. I'm just about to tell him to get lost... When I suddenly find myself locked into his soft brown eyes that take take command of me for a moment. With an effort I break away shaking my head clearing the fuzziness within. 'Thank you — but, no, it's complicated.' I reply my head still buzzing.

'Aren't they all.' He replies the tone of his voice now sounded softer, almost melodic.

'Besides...' I reply looking up finding myself once more staring into the soft friendly smiling eyes. I try to speak but the words just won't come out. His eyes are so alluring. So hypnotic. 'I...' It is a effort to think, let alone talk. I'm completely unable to form any words. 'I...' It takes a real force of will. 'I don't even know you.' I finally manage to respond forcing out an objection.

'*All the better*,' He replies giving a smile, his voice now almost a whisper. '*I'm a total stranger, who is both completely impartial and a good listener, or — so I'm told.*'

At this I begin laughing, this was just too weird. 'Who the hell are you?'

'*Well. Don't tell anyone but.*' His head darts comically around the still empty bar scanning for any eavesdroppers. He then leans forward slightly beckoning me to do the same. What the heck, I inwardly shrug then lean forward conspiratorially our heads are only inches apart. '*You see,*' he whispers. '*I'm your guardian angel and I'm here to help in your time of personal crisis.*'

CHAPTER 2

I remain silent for a moment there is a solemn quality to his statement that is, almost convincing. 'That's really good' I sit back laughing. 'My own personal guardian angel? Just like James Stewart had in It's a wonderful life? Alright, I admit it's a great line. But, it fails on two counts.'

'Only two?' He looks at me incredulous. 'I must be getting better at this job. Okay. What are they?'

'Firstly,' I reply holding up a finger. 'It's not quite Christmas, you're over a week early. And second,' I say holding up a second finger. 'I'm betting your name's not Clarence.'

He grins *'I guess you've got me on both counts. That said, I will let you into a couple of guardian angel secrets. Firstly,'* he holds up a finger. *'We don't just appear around Christmas. It's a 24/7, 52 weeks of the year deal. And second,'* he holds up a second finger. *As strange as it may seem. Not all guardian angels are called Clarence.'*

'I suppose not, that would get quite confusing.' Then I glance at my watch which reads 10 pm, I could head off home, not an attractive prospect. Or, my eyes return to the waiting glass. What to do?

As if once again he is able to read my mind the decision is made for me as he picks up the glass of bourbon and places it to the side. 'What are you doing?' I asked annoyed.

ONE HOUR: TOTAL SURRENDER

'*Providing you with a third choice*,' he replies instructing the bartender who grunts an acknowledgement then heads off to the coffee machine. '*I'm ordering us some coffee and getting ready to hear your story.*'

'You're really are quite persistent, what if I say NO and get l...' His eyes glow with a soft haze and I am suddenly unable to speak I experience a brief moment where I feel I can tell him absolutely anything.

'*I'd be a pretty poor guardian angel if I were dissuaded so easily now, wouldn't I?*' As he speaks his eyes seem to glow with increased intensity. '*Plus, you could put me out of a job. And — you wouldn't want that now. Would you?*' His voice is a whisper yet sounds inside my head. I find myself staring deeper into his hypnotic glowing soft brown eyes as each word resonates deep within me '*Plus, you could put me out of a job. And — you wouldn't want that now. Would you?*' His words echo softly in my mind gently bouncing around like a tennis ball in slow motion repeating over and over. '*Plus, you could put me out of a job. And — you wouldn't want that now. Would you? Would you?—Would you?*' It is impossible to resist. The room dims around us. For a moment I have a deep sense that there is no one and nothing except the two of us inside some sort of dark void. The bar suddenly reappears around me I am conscious that a few more people are seated near the door, strange how I never even saw or sensed them enter.

'No, no you're quite right, I...I really—couldn't have that.' I say mystified at what just happened.

The coffee's arrive, the bartender sets them down then heads off to serve some people who have just walked in. The stranger picks up a cup places it in front of me sits back and waits. Once again I face his soft patient gaze, this is too weird, I tell myself but, what the heck. 'I don't even know your name, guardian angel.'

Taking a sip of his coffee he regards me for a moment. '*My apologies, I overlook my manners. It's Nathaniel. As I said, not all guardian angels are called Clarence.*' He replies holding out a large hand. Taking it I am conscious how small mine is in comparison, his grip is firm but curiously gentle as I experience a mild electrical shock that runs up my arm and right through me causing my entire being to resonate momentarily like a tuning fork.

'It's good to meet you, Nathaniel.' I hear myself saying with a realisation that he hasn't at any time asked my name. My hand is still in his, it takes a real act of will to break away and recover it. My cheeks burn as I do so. Once again I mentally kick myself for acting like a silly shy little school girl in his presence.

I can feel myself shaking inside as I take a sip of my coffee, using the moment to compose myself while glancing up at the patient Nathaniel. 'So tell me.' I pause for a moment still questioning if I should continue interacting with this man. 'Just how does this guardian angel thing work?'

'*I beg your pardon.*' Nathaniel responds with a furrowed brow.

'How exactly does this guardian angel thing work?' I take another sip of coffee then give him a steely glare the sort I use in the court room when cross examining a witness or during a deposition. A smile slowly appears as he places his cup down followed by a laugh.

ONE HOUR: TOTAL SURRENDER

'Oh that is good Justine. Do you know in all the years I've been doing this, and it has been for quite some time. I can honestly say, I've never once been asked anything like that before. But it's a fair question. And one I should have anticipated from a lawyer.'

I bristle for a moment. 'How do you know my name and that I'm a lawyer?' I blurt.

'Elementary my dear Justine. This bar is a haunt for lawyers, that and the way you are dressed tells me you are a lawyer. But, the real teller? The real teller is the business card in your purse.' He points to my bag that sits on the bar to my left with my wallet poking out the top openly displaying my business and credit cards. How did...? I was certain it was secured in a pocket.

'Okay, Sherlock. You got me.' I find myself laughing despite my surprise, placing the wallet back in my bag securing the zipper on the pocket.

'If it helps, I can assure you we are bound by a sort of celestial non disclosure agreement and an exceptionally, strict code of conduct.'

'Okay. I suppose, I'm sufficiently reassured by that. So where do I start?'

'At the beginning Justine, continue, until you come to the end — then stop.' Before I can reply his eyes glow again but this time with an intensity of a very light green. *'Don't hold back on any detail. Tell me everything. Every — thing.'* My head bobs confirming the instruction.

'He,' I begin, 'I mean James was my first.' I pause again my mind was racing. He had indeed been my first in so many ways. First proper boy friend, first man I had ever made love to. Not some sweaty inexperienced fumble in the back of a car, like after the Prom with Billy Curtis, I'd so wanted Billy to be my first back then. There we were in the back of his car my dress up my panties sodden with desire. I was so wanting it. Billy desperately unzipping his fly, his rapid breathing on my neck, then that fateful pause and groan as he came in his pants from over excitement. I had just laid silent in a frustrated rage. I felt the burning flush in my cheeks return. 'I, I had never...' I became surprisingly flustered.

'*I understand.*' Came Nathaniel's soothing voice as he places his hand gently upon mine, something that I found welcome even, reassuring. It just seemed to cut through all the doubts within. '*He was your first in many ways wasn't he?*' Again I found myself nodding in confirmation. '*What happened then?*'

I paused recalling past events, we moved in together after law school, secured good jobs, I thought we were happy, that was until earlier today. 'I'd gone to James's office to surprise him by taking him to lunch, his secretary told me he hadn't been in, that he'd rang in sick. I knew that wasn't right as he had left for the office just before me and had appeared fine. So I tried to call him on his cell and got no answer nor at home where he was supposed to be. So I went home to check on him and...'

'*And?*' Nathaniel asked taking another sip of coffee, his brown eyes now seemed to bore right into me.

'I arrived home to find...' I walked into our home to find it had been cleared out. For a moment I feared we had been burgled and was about to call the police. Then I realised that only his stuff was gone. Clothes, belongings everything... The letter that he'd left on the side table was short and to the point. He just could not go on living a lie anymore, he was deeply unhappy. We both wanted totally different things in life, there was so much more to life than career chasing he had said. I felt the anger bubble as I had read the letter. But he was right. He'd tried to tell me so many times and —I just hadn't listened. I'd always being too busy. Too busy working on a new case, or going to another meeting. Or heading off on another course. All centred towards chasing my dream of making partner with the firm. Ultimately. Was it any wonder James left me?

'So *here you are all alone on a Friday night.*' Nathaniel whispers. '*Blaming yourself for your failed relationship.*'

'Exactly, feeling like a complete failure and telling my troubles to a total stranger.'

'*Sounds to me like you needed to tell someone.*'

'This is insane' I exclaim placing the cup down hard on the saucer causing it to clatter.

'*What is? Your problem or sitting here talking to me?*'

'Both.'

'*I suppose so,*' Nathaniel concedes. '*But at least this way you're addressing the issue, rather than running away from it.*' Gesturing to the Bourbon glass

'Running away how?' I growl.

'*As I said earlier,*' he places the glass in front of me. '*One double bourbon, then maybe another or two or more? You get to forget about it all for a brief period. Then you wake up tomorrow feeling like crap. After which, it starts all over again. Nothing is resolved.*'

'I guess you're right.' I conceded.

'*You're a lot smarter than that.*'

'So tell me guardian angel, what do I do now?' I ask finishing my coffee.

'*What do you want to do?*' Nathaniel asks leaning forward a little. 'You are the author of your own happiness and future, isn't time to start a new chapter?' 'His eyes seem to sparkle as he speaks, it is both reassuring and yet — mysteriously seductive also. The aching in my breasts returns with renewed emphasis. Why was I reacting to him so?

'*Would you...*' He trails off for a moment as if carefully considering his next words. '*Would you care to continue our conversation, somewhere more comfortable and—private?*' His brown eyes glow, once again I cannot break his gaze. My nipples grow painfully hard as he speaks '*Do — say yes Justine.*'

At his words an insane resolve possesses me. Screw you James. Screw you! Breaking away from his gaze. I glance down at the glass, grab it, then, to Nathaniel's clear surprise I down its contents in one. The liquid hits me like a sledge hammer, causing me to c— cough, I give out a silly raspy laugh. Then place the glass down with a thud upon the counter, I pause for a moment then turn to him. 'You live far from here guardian angel?' I hear myself ask confidently.

'*Not far. Not far at all.*'

'Good. Because I don't feel like going home tonight.'

Nathaniel gives a nod of understanding, stands, then places some notes on the bar, before helping me on with my coat. We leave the bar stepping out into the bitterly cold Chicago night air and hail a cab 'Do you live alone? I feel the liquor now taking effect leaving me a little light headed along with the biting cold night wind feel my face flush.

'*I'm a confirmed bachelor Guardian Angel.*' Nathaniel replies softly opening the cab door, without hesitation I climb in.

CHAPTER 3

The cab drops us off outside of a large house on the corner of a dimly lit street, somewhere in the southern part of Chicago, I couldn't be certain but I was sure I'd spotted a sign stating Mount Greenwood as we drove off the main road. I step out of the cab into the biting wind then follow him up to the front door of a large house. He slid the key in the lock then turns to me. *'I apologise in advance for the untidiness of my home I've only recently moved in.'* Following him in behind I step through the door into a large hall, it is quite bare except for a small table just to the left of the doorway upon which is a small silver tray where Nathaniel deposits his house keys into it with a loud "Ching." To my front is a wide elegant creamy white wooden stair case with ornate carvings on the banisters, the stair case ascends upwards then branches around to the left and right leading on to a beautiful light cream landing that led to the bedrooms. As my gaze reaches the top I catch the reflected dancing lights on the top wall from a magnificent chandelier that hangs at the top. I catch my breath at the sheer beauty of the stairs and chandelier, that brings visions of great houses such as the fictional of Tara in the book and movie of "Gone with the Wind." I imagine Scarlet O'Hara and Rhett Butler descending the staircase hand in hand. *'It's so beautiful.'* I hear myself whisper.

'Thank you. It needs quite a bit of work but,yes, it is a lovely house.' With that Nathaniel beckons me to follow and we head through a door into a beautiful large dining hall the walls are of a dark mahogany panelling that had clearly seen better days, there are cracks and lose pieces of wood hang limp and sad, the flooring is a black and white square tiling effect, that reminds me of a large chess board. The over head light shone alone and dimly as the only just about working of three bulbs and curiously a metal hook hung menacingly from the ceiling in the centre of the room with two large metal rings secured into the floor . To the far side of the room are two white French doors with thick dark felt curtains covered in a thin layer of dust either side.

We move through into a smaller room and I'm soon sitting on a comfy sofa in Nathaniel's fairly bare lounge a small dark brown coffee table just a few yards away. Glancing around the room, there are no pictures hanging anywhere in the room, some rather tatty looking drapes hang over the window, and against the far wall I catch sight of a beautiful Grandfather clock in dark wood the dial indicating 11.40.

Nathaniel enters with a tray of coffee then places it on the small table. He sits down next to me his brown eyes brush across my face. I swear I can actually feel his eyes travelling down the length of my body with a softness of a caress; running up my legs, they hover briefly on the ankles, then my thighs. I suck in an involuntary breath, the sensation is almost, as if he were gently stroking over my body with his fingertips. The warmth ascends as his eyes move up over my hips and on to my full breasts, where they linger for a bit. I feel myself take another deep breath as my nipples harden as if on command of his gaze. I feel an unusual ache as they protrude through the thin material of my bra and blouse. Much more pronounced than the effect he had on me in the bar.

Nathaniel holds his gaze for a moment then places his coffee cup on the table leans forward and gently takes my hand, for a brief moment I don't know what to do or say. As if reading my mind he gently takes the cup from my hand, and with out breaking eye contact places it gently on the small table. Then he bends forward a little more lightly strokes my face, it feels amazingly gentle, I close my eyes for a moment as he does so allowing the sensation to flow through me and linger. How long had it been since I had even come close to feeling anything like this? Though the question hung in mid air only for a moment before vanishing.

Opening my eyes I find myself looking into his, falling slowly into those soft hypnotic brown orbs my will slowly dissolves, overcome by a light dizziness and warmth, his face begins to blur in and out of focus. With a jolt, the room suddenly felt like it was beginning to revolve slowly around me, then begins picking up speed a moment of panic seizes me, alarmed I try to stand but my rubbery legs barely support me. 'Whoa, whoa...' I hear myself as I sway uncontrollably he gently grabs my waist pulls me back down to the sofa.

I try to form words but nothing comes out. 'Shhhhh don't try to speak.' His voice is soft and commanding. 'Just lie back, that's it.' Unable to resist I obey his instructions the couch feels so soft yielding to my form like — a soft cloud as I lie back against the cushions. The spinning comes to a stop with a sudden jolt. His gentle voice seems to sound in my mind. *'Don't be afraid*

Justine. I've brought you into my realm, you'll feel a little strange but all is fine. You are completely safe. We can spend some time together here.'

His realm…What was he talking about? Disorientated I close my eyes for a moment to try and overcome the dizziness that I am experiencing then open them to see Nathaniel crouch down then gently lift my legs up and place my ankles on the raised end of the couch. Then raising a leg, he slowly and gently removes a shoe places it on the floor, pauses for a moment before starting to massage the foot through the soft material of my stocking. His thumbs press gently but firmly into the ball of my foot expertly working the pressure points. *'Oh that's so good',* I hear myself whisper. All tension within me literally falls away as his fingers and especially thumbs gently stroke, press and probe up along the sole of my foot. It was, simply put — exquisite. I am captive to his magical fingers that just rob me of all strength and will. He pauses for a moment then places the foot down, before gently lifting the other leg removes the other shoe slowly, very — slowly. The tension is almost unbearable I find myself willing him to hurry as the shoe is eventually removed, my foot then begins to receive the same treatment as the other had. Another deep breath follows, I start biting my lower lip as his fingers press firmly into the sole creating spiralling bright colours and images in my mind that I have never before encountered.

'Does that feel good?' his whisper cuts through the swirling colours and incredible sensations. Unable to speak I can just about focus enough to give a nod in acknowledgement. A warm flush runs through my body, nipples tighten into dagger points and begin to ache, wetness flushes between my legs.

All this—just from his touch.

ONE HOUR: TOTAL SURRENDER

Fingers slide up my leg lifting the hem of my skirt to the top of my stocking.

He begins to roll the stocking down sliding it off the leg, the cool air seems to kiss the bare skin forcing me to take another deep breath. He begins to stroke the leg, it feels so good. His fingers glide up and down with a gentleness I never imagined possible.

Fingernails gently scratch either side of the leg sending a sustained jolt of electrical like charge throughout my body that jerks and stiffens by something that feels almost orgasmic.

Then I am rigid. My entire body seems to remain held fast for what feels like an ages before I become limp and experience a free falling sensation dropping with a soft "Flmmff" into the embracing softness of the sofa. I'm breathing rapidly, my breasts so hot with arousal. Then, the other stocking is gently removed, causing me to gasp again as he repeats what he had done before, the nails lightly scratching the either side of leg once more forcing me to go rigid for what seems longer than before. When the release comes there is once again the sensation of free falling from a height, only this time I'm falling for sometime before impacting with another soft "Flmmff" and being embraced once again into the complete soft reassuring embrace of the sofa. My mind is a whirl overwhelmed with a myriad of incredible colours, my body aroused beyond anything I have every imagined possible, my breasts heave rapidly. He takes hold of my arms places them down on my stomach crossing them at the wrists. Something soft is wrapped around them and secured in a slow even pressure. Opening my eyes is an effort, lifting my head is almost impossible I just manage to do so focusing long enough to see that he has bound my wrists together with one of my stockings. 'What...' my words were cut off with a gentle finger to my lips followed by a '*Shhhh.*' Slumping back on the soft cushion I am so weak totally unable to resist as he raises my bound arms up over my head, I try to pull them away but have no strength there is a small jerk as they are secured to something.

'Nathaniel, I ...' Another finger to my lips, '*Shhhh.*' Then something soft brushes against them. '*Open.*' One whispered, yet a soft overwhelmingly powerful command. I obey opening my mouth to feel something soft placed between my teeth, it smells and tastes of...Stocking. Surprised at the realisation I bite down upon the material only to discover he has tied a large knot in it that now completely fills my mouth. Then he gently parts my hair at the base of my neck ties it tight gagging me muting any sounds I might make. I try to rally what residual of strength I have remaining, to protest but all that comes out is pathetic whimper. What was wrong with me? I feel so weak, yet — so incredibly horny also.

Tugging at my wrists is futile they remain secure, in any case I have no strength. The gag in my mouth is now causing me to drool a little. I'm totally helpless, unable to resist in any way. Just like a damsel on TV, bound, gagged and at the mercy of her kinky captor. The thought causes another wet flush between my legs, a dark memory of watching a woman in a detective series captured by the bad guy. He had her tied tightly her mouth stuffed with a thick scarf and all she could do was writhe about helplessly as he gloated over her. How that had turned me on, I had unconsciously touched myself watching fantasising what it would be like for the captor to take his pleasure as my body betrays my real feelings in Total contradiction to my struggles and protests.

ONE HOUR: TOTAL SURRENDER

Now here I was and it is no fantasy as his hands begin to explore my body. His touch is so light delicately stroking the sides of my ribs, hips, thighs, lightly brushing my breasts. Then my neck and hair, his fingers so delicate they seem to arouse everywhere they touch. The gag just mutes my pitiful sounds, I'm too weak, to do anything other than just react to his touch. And yet — he just continues to explore me, touching, driving me wild with the tips of his soft fingers.

Nathaniel was playing me like a musical instrument, as expertly as a maestro. His hands stop at my hips the zipper of my skirt is then gently pulled down before unfastening the the waist hooks, effortlessly lifting my hips he slides the skirt down my legs before depositing it on the floor. The last Button of the blouse is unfastened then the folds are parted to reveal my heaving breasts cradled in the light blue bra. Nathaniel takes an audible breath of pure delight at the sight of them strokes the bare skin causing me to shiver and gasp as yet more small electrical like charges shoot through my body.

His hands started to stroke my firm mounds, caressing them, molding and reshaping them with an audible growl of satisfaction. Nathaniel then stands regarding me silently as I lay breathing rapidly my slit so wet, clit throbbing, nipples rigid and aching, my whole body wanton with desire, right then and there I wanted him inside me and yet — he just stood watching me. Arching my back I force myself to raise my hips, begging through the gag I cried out, I didn't care if I was acting like some wanton slut. My whole being screamed: *"For God's sake! Fuck Me!"*

Nathaniel smiles gives a nod of understanding, before starting to unbutton his shirt painfully slowly, making me wait causing me to moan more then lift my hips again I desperately needed fucking. Never in my life have I been like this. I didn't care. Nothing mattered except wanting him inside me. Take me. Take me Now!

After what seems like an eternity Nathaniel slowly removes his shirt revealing a muscled torso, strong arms and a very manly hairy chest.

Next, he kicks off his shoes, unbuckles his belt unfastens the waist band of his pants slips them off followed his boxer shorts. His large cock stood erect the pink glans protruding glistening in the light.

As I fight to focus my only thought is how large it is. I feel a sting of panic, for a moment mind screams I can't possibly take him. As my eyes meet his again the panic just dissolves. Replaced by the simple need that I can't wait any longer, he is torturing me by holding back, no more.

No More. Please!

A smile appears on Nathaniel's face one of understanding the pleading in my eyes.

Then, he begins to glow with a soft white luminescence, much like I had witnessed in his eyes. The bright white luminescence grows in intensity to almost blinding, I have to close to my eyes it is so overpowering. In a moment the light recedes bathing Nathaniel in its soft embrace as he remains standing silent for a moment. Then to my horror a pair of large white feathery wings start to sprout from the tops of his muscled shoulders extending out at an angle of about 45 degrees growing upwards and down until they open wide and begin to flap very slowly creating a slight cooling breeze. Nathaniel stands before me in the ball of light, naked with protruding wings, gorgeous white feathers with burnt black tips that run along the top and outer edges, the lower tips of which reach down almost to his ankles.

As I stare at the vision before me my mind races, unable to comprehend. Nathaniel moves slowly towards me looming over my bound form like a colossus.

Curiously I don't register any weight as he slowly climbs on top of me, only a reassuring softness and warmth followed by the most incredible sensation as he enters me effortlessly pausing for a moment as I feel him deep within.

Followed by the intense sensation of being fucked into into another realm.

At last — I am his.

That is the last I recall as everything faded into blackness.

CHAPTER 4

I awaken with a start to a sensation of moving and rocking motions of being in some sort of vehicle. Regaining my senses I realise that I am in the back of some sort of car. No, a cab. I literally have no recollection of how I got here. I sit up a little too quickly and immediately regret it as the dizziness hits. I close my eyes for a moment allowing it to subside sufficiently to take stock. Glancing ahead through the windshield I note that it is still quite dark. Then note the driver's photo and licence on the dash to my front.

My mind is foggy, my whole body resonates with a strange static like charge and euphoria.

The last thing I remember was being with Nathaniel, his touch. Oh, his touch...

At that very moment the cab comes to a halt. 'We're here lady.' The cab driver declares, glancing over nervously at me

'Here?' I mumble coming out of my fog of pleasure, then looking around trying to make sense of the situation. 'Here? Where?'

The driver turns and gives me a quizzical look 'Where you asked to go, 475 Laycome. That'll be 14.50.'

'Where, I...' I recognise we are outside my house but I don't recall getting into the cab let alone instructing him where to take me. 'Yes, yes of course, I'm so sorry, been a long day.' I mumble not very convincingly. I glance at my watch it reads 12.50. No. No. That couldn't be right. Then glanced at the drivers dashboard it read 12.51. No. That simply wasn't possible.

The driver regards me silently for a moment, 'Are you sure you're okay miss?'

'What? Yes, thank you,' I say handing him twenty as my mind is doing cartwheels. 'Keep the change.'

'Sure he replies smiling.'

My legs barely support me as I exit the cab, then stagger like a drunk towards my door. Letting myself in I close the door with my butt, then fall back against it sliding down into a heap.

What the hell just happened to me? Everything is a blur. The bar, yes, I recalled the bar, meeting Nathaniel, then... Going back to his home, yes. Having coffee — then...I am overwhelmed with... flashes of Images, Disjointed, Chaotic and yet... So Intense.

***'You're so beautiful Justine, so very beautiful.'* His voice is a soft whisper that seems so distant my body is literally on fire, mild electric shocks the emanate from his finger tips. Shocks that zip directly into my breasts causing a delicious burning that extends to my already erect nipples. Within this ecstatic maelstrom the only conscious thought in my mind is that I want him —I need him inside me.**

I find myself back from the vision still slumped against the front door. Something prompts me to reach into my coat pocket, I touch something soft then remove it to discover it is the remnants of — my panties. Followed by my stockings, or rather one of them, one with a large knot tied in the middle, still wet from my saliva. Searching the other pockets I can find no sign of the other stocking, or my bra. What the hell had happened to me?

Forcing myself up I manage to stagger up the stairs to the bathroom, switching on the shower I undress then examined myself in the mirror, I looked a mess my hair, and make up. But my body has been through quite a session, I am covered in bruises on my wrists, arms, ankles and chest. Were those bite marks on my shoulder? I step inside the shower hot cascading water embraces me, as I start to soap myself. In that moment the pain eases. I feel alive and invigorated, the soap sets off mild electrical charges all over my skin, particularly between my legs and nipples My fingers began to probe into my sex I'm so wet. So very wet, so very aroused.

Swept up in the experience I have a aching need to. It feels so good, like nothing I have felt before when pleasuring myself, something I confess, aside from earlier in the cab, I hadn't indulged in quite a while. Yes, I'd enjoyed it at college but not so much now. Work always took precedence, there's always a new project or contract to deal with. I just didn't have the time... Right now though, nothing else mattered the compulsion is irresistible as my soapy fingers slide over my gorged clit making me gasp first working up and down at first, then round and round adding a little pressure. The climax hits me like I had run fast into a brick wall. I slump back against the shower screen then Slide down the glass partition into a heap breathless, exhausted but, Oh, so very satisfied.

After drying myself I sprawl out on my bed and nod off for a few hours. When I awaken I need to go again. Reaching into my bedside table I pull out a small plastic bag. It had been a gift from James who had wanted help me to relax more after work. The black Hitachi wand seemed to glow in the dim light of the bedside lamp, in a moment it is plugged into the wall socket then switched on. A low hum emanates from the wand my need growing evermore by the second my body tenses, then relaxes as the head of the vibrating wand dances lightly over my aching slit...

I awaken laid out on my bed, breathless, my entire body on heat, a sheen covers my breasts and chest. I'm constantly on heat as a result.

My faithful Hitachi takes the brunt of my endless need.

CHAPTER 5

Monday, I'm in my office utterly exhausted, and completely unable to focus. The endless meetings are a jumble of meaningless discussions, figures and graphs. Nothing makes any sense or for that matter is of any consequence. Ever since my encounter with Nathaniel, I find myself in a constant state of preoccupation and despite the bruises, my body is in a constant state of need. My inability to listen is immediately picked up by two of the partners. I fail to register questions being put to me. The Rowlands Contract is due to be signed a multi million dollar project I was given to head up and complete before Christmas. When asked as to whether it is ready, I am unable to answer, my mind is so fuzzy. The room is silent, Jerrod Conners one of the senior partners gives a look that is daggers. The meeting ends everyone leaves seemingly in a hurry and I left alone with Jerrod and Mike Crowthorn another senior partner. I'm hauled over the coals for being off my game. 'Get a grip of yourself Justine.' Conners says. 'You are a rising star with this firm and if you hope to make partner, as I know you do. You need to get focused regardless of the fact it is Christmas. I want that contract in the bag' Crowthorn adds a few unhelpful comments then storms out.

ONE HOUR: TOTAL SURRENDER

I just sit silent as Conners gives me a pep talk about getting a grip, I'm a senior member of staff with a stellar career ahead of me. I truly don't recall most of it and left his office wondering for the first time if, after all my hard work, this is what I truly wanted out of life? The thought was brief but it shocked me.

'Ms Preston?' I'm suddenly jolted out of my thoughts by a voice. 'You okay Ms Preston?'

My P.A. Ryan stands before me, for the first time I consciously find myself taking in every inch of his tall muscular form.

'It's none of my business I know,' Comes his soft southern accent. But you seem a little distracted.'

I almost snap at him for being so presumptuous, with a: "How dare you." Which is instantly replaced by a softer response of: 'Thanks for your concern Ryan. I'm fine just a little preoccupied.'

'Sure,' he replies not at all convinced. 'I've brought the Rowlands contracts for you, Mr Conners told me you were going to finalise them.'

'Leave them on my desk, thank you.' He nods then places the file down. As I watch him leave it occurs to me that I couldn't recall, how long he'd been working for me now. Six months? A year? Longer? Through my fogged brain a voice within shouts out: "One year and two months to be exact, ever since you were promoted." And yet, only now was I looking him over and acknowledging the effect he had on me. Of course I had noticed him before and yes, I confess to having had fleeting fantasies about him. There was a strong rumour that Helen Chambers, the predatory head of accounts most certainly knew having spirited him away to the board room on level 6 during last years Christmas party. I couldn't help but feel a strong pang of envy.

Ryan is younger than me, early 20's standing an impressive 6, 3, with a strong athletic body and a firm sexy butt. And my thoughts about him at this moment are anything but fleeting or professional. As I glance over the paperwork he had left I'm still unable to focus, not only am I truly am off my usual game; but noises carry from down the hall through into my office, laughing and the feint tuneless attempts at a Christmas carol or two, along with more laughing.

Here I was working as everyone else began to celebrate, the firm Christmas party was beginning. But then, what was there for me to celebrate or be happy about? James would be spending the holidays doing lord knows what. And I— I would be spending it alone. Well maybe not completely alone — there was always my faithful Hitachi.

But that was not enough. The intensity of the visions had left me in a state constant need, and boy was I in need right now. The thought whizzed through my mind causing an instant of surprise that vanished in a second to be replaced by one simple fact. I Needed Fucking.

As if in response to that thought, Ryan entered my office holding two glasses of champagne smiling wished me a Merry Christmas asked if I was coming to join the party?

'Sure Ryan, thank you.' I hear myself reply, glancing up from the paperwork, surprised by his consideration. 'Have a seat I'll be done in moment.' My voice is surprisingly soft and to be honest, I am quite moved by his kindness.

ONE HOUR: TOTAL SURRENDER

'Okay.' He replies then sits almost facing me silently sipping his drink. I pretended to still be perusing the contract, but all I can do is keep glancing over the rim of my glasses taking in the line of his powerful legs, his strong neck and that dark hair, I catch a feint whiff of his spicy cologne.

I imagine he is checking me out silently, his eyes sweeping gently over me, my heart is beating rapidly with desire. As I glance back down to the contract a strange sensation sweeps over me as he checks me out, I can actually feel his eyes on me, lightly brushing my face, I shiver then experience my hair being brushed away lightly to reveal an ear another shiver. It's as if his finger tips are brushing the lobe edge I took a deep breath closing my eyes for a second, forcing myself to focus. Then, it continues along my neck a sensation of light sensual kisses, followed by a light nibbling of my ear. I allow the sensations to continue until...I simply can't take anymore. Placing the pen down as gently as I can, I slowly stand then without a word make my way from my desk over to the door of my office push it closed then turn handle engaging the lock it with an audible click. Pausing for dramatic effect keeping my back to him for a few moments before removing my hands from the door take a deep breath before quickly unfastening a button or two on my blouse to reveal a little cleavage, then turn slowly to face him. Ryan stares at at me mouth agape. 'Something wrong — Ms Preston?' He mumbles nervously as I face him.

'No. There's nothing wrong. Nothing at all Ryan. I just want to make sure, we're not disturbed. You don't mind if we have the party here— do you?' I find myself reply in a whisper as I slowly advance towards him. *'How long have you been my P.A. now?*

I ask picking up the spare Champagne glass, then remove my glasses and place them down. I chink his glass with mine as he holds it up almost like a shield before him.

'I, I don't know... Just over a year, I think Ms Preston.' The young man stammers not sure what is going on.

'Very good. *It's actually just over 14 months now. And it's — Justine*,' I whisper taking a step forward so we are only inches apart as I gently taking his hand. '*Say it.*'

'Say. I don't... I don't understand.'

'*My name Ryan. Say my name. None of that—Ms Preston crap.*'

'*Justine, I...*' There is an almost terrified look in his eyes as I stand just inches from him my chest heaving his eyes glance down to my cleavage then back up, his cheeks flush.

'*Say it, again*,' I whisper the command in his ear my warm breath causes him to visibly shiver.

'*Justine.*' Comes the breathless reply, the fear that was in his eyes is now more confusion.

'*That's good Ryan, I've wanted you to say my name for so long now. Say it again.*' I whisper placing my glass down.

'*Justine, I've...*'

'*Shhhh*,' I say placing a finger to his lips, then take the glass from his hand finish the contents in one gulp before placing it down, then reaching up I begin to slowly remove his jacket, he makes no effort to protest or resist as it glides back over his shoulders and slips to the floor. Locking eyes I start to unfasten his tie, once free a gentle constant pull and it slides off from his neck, to be deposited on the floor with his jacket. He takes a few rapid breaths as I slowly unbutton his shirt.

ONE HOUR: TOTAL SURRENDER

'*You want me — don't you Ryan?*' The young man makes to speak but is prevented by my placing a finger to his lips once more. '*It's okay. I know, you do. That's not at all appropriate — for a P.A. to have such thoughts or desires for his boss.*'

The young mans eyes widen as I take his hand gently then place it on my right breast. With that he gently squeezed then made small circles with his palm lightly grazing my nipple

'*It's not at all appropriate for a P.A. to think or act so.*' I whisper in his ear. '*But it is — for a lover.*'

At this our mouths meet hungrily.

CHAPTER 6

Ever since the office Christmas party a few days ago, I've been been in a literal tail spin over my conduct with Ryan. Looking back it is like I am observing a total stranger, only one who is the exact image of me.

What the hell had I been thinking throwing myself at him like that? I had allowed my deep need to completely dominate me. That's not to say though, that it had in anyway been a disappointment. Oh No.

Once he had overcome his initial shock and, with a little encouragement, he had taken me on my desk. I had, had such a need for him to take me. But not before his mouth had worked its magic between my legs my wet slit had cried out for attention and he had obliged in a very enthusiastic way, a little instruction and...He had become a God of intense pleasure with his mouth, his tongue swirling around my clit whilst his fingers moved in circles and piston like within driving me almost insane. He had removed his fingers then had literally fucked me with his tongue, whilst his now dripping wet fingers made circles of varying pressures upon my clit.

It had been amazing.

After as I lay on my desk panting recovering from the aftershocks my blouse open his head appeared between my legs above the hem of my hiked skirt, my juices running down his face, his lips and chin glistened. Climbing on me our mouths met the taste of my juices only served to excite me more I now wanted him inside me so much, but he'd climbed off. leaving me perplexed. 'What...?'

I never got to finish as he took a hand pulled me roughly off the table, his eyes wide with a primal desire, I even caught an almost cave man like growl as he did so. Before I could utter a sound I was spun around and roughly shoved face down over my desk, my skirt was hiked up more, his hard cock rubbed and throbbed against my bare butt. For a moment I thought he was going to take me anal, and I confess part of me had even wished he did. My heart raced in anticipation, then I cry out as my head is jerked back as he grabs my hair. Bending close behind me, he snarls in my ear 'My turn now, Ms Preston. No more Justine's lover.' His voice is deep and commanding. 'No. Now, I'm just going to fuck my dirty little slut of a boss.' Another hard jerk of my hair, then he takes me from behind, I gasp as he just slides into me I'm so aroused there is no resistance. I feel him deep inside, he pauses for a while savouring the moment, then begins to fuck me, long and slow. I could feel him becoming more and more excited as he took me giving my hair a tug every so often making me yelp. As he lived out his fantasy of ramming and dominating his slut boss.

But I confess— I loved it. I absolutely fucking loved giving in to his fantasy and—if truth be told a deep secret one of mine. Not that I would have ever admitted it. In the past I found such thoughts dirty, unfit for a lady to have. Now however. Now I no longer cared. Being taken in my office was so hot and whilst the party went on just down the corridor.

Ryan became so excited that he began fucking me like a battering ram. It was so raw, his vocalisations were almost cave man. I heard myself moan in pleasure, I knew his climax was building, his breathing and frantic strokes spoke volumes, just as he was about to come — he withdrew, exploding all over my butt. Then he massaged his cum in with one hand before giving my hair a good tug with the other hand bringing head back then forcing me to lick his fingers clean. 'Like a good little slut boss should,' he whispered.

But it had not ended there, I then knelt in front of him, took hold of his semi erect cock still dripping with my juices and cum and gently brushed the tip against my lips. Looking up into his eyes there was a flicker of a smile as I took him in my mouth tongue swirling around my mouth bringing him erect again. After which he had taken me again. Only, this time — as I wanted. The Dirty Slut Boss was back in charge. I wanted him to take me against the wall of my office, my legs wrapped tightly around his waist. He had pounded me banging the wall with regular Thud. Thud. Thud!

It was so very raw.

So Primal.

So Fucking Amazing.

Afterwards we lay together on the office couch it felt so good and safe to be in his strong arms and the reassuring firmness of his virile body. Later after cleaning ourselves up, we joined the party enjoying the drinks, joking, even singing a few carols and for the first time in — I can't remember how long, I had truly enjoyed myself, totally forgetting my sadness and James. Later after saying good night to Ryan, I took a cab home having had a fair bit to drink, I felt good and after having been royally fucked by Ryan I crashed out utterly exhausted on my bed only to be hit by the most vivid dream.

I am kneeling on a hard bare wooden floor my blouse is gently pulled down my arms from behind, the clasp of my bra is released and it slides down my arms onto the floor. I am on all fours the stocking gag still tight in my mouth, drool running down the sides of my mouth. My skirt is hiked up, fingers slide down the base of my back under the waistband of my panties, there is a feeling of tension in the panties as the fingers grip the material, a quick twist and the remnant material is dropped to the floor. My inner thighs are softly slapped open for him to enter unencumbered. He does so, gently taking his time as I experience his slow glide within. He remains still for a moment, a hand cups a breast squeezing it as just he begins to pull back and thrust. Then my hair is grabbed with a jerk, causing me to cry out that is muffled by the gag. His thrusts gather speed sending me into a maelstrom of building orgasm as it begins rolling with increased momentum towards its zenith, more flashes, then his fingers are on my clit, taking it between forefinger and thumb he exerts a slow pressure.

Oh my God!

My entire being explodes.

I awaken in a sweat, the experience is almost overwhelming, I lay quiet unable to move, my mind races. What has happened to me? I've become such a wanton slut. I also can't believe my tardiness at work, my inability to get a fucking grip. During the party Jerrod Connors had pulled me aside briefly wanting the Rowlands contract. I'd retrieved it from my office then handed it to him, the same contract that I had not completed checking. The same contract that had been swept onto the floor of my office along with everything else that had been on my desk when Ryan and I had made love. He thanks me as he is now able to conclude the negotiations and seal the deal, a great boost for the firm and another step forward for me towards becoming a partner. To be honest, I truly did not care anymore. I was still unable to focus, still so constantly in need. No matter how I tried to reason nothing made sense.

I needed answers. And only one person could provide them. I resolve to get them.

I enter the bar before it starts to get busy, I quickly make my way to a corner seat where I could observe the front door, whilst remaining out of sight, slowly over time the bar begins to fill. People drink, laugh and celebrate, piped Christmas music helps to get everyone into the holiday spirit. I had debated all day whether to go through with this but I know I have no option now. Sitting in the bar, I order another mineral water and continued working on my phone, answering emails and texts whilst observing the coming and goings. Glancing at my watch I note I'd been here over two hours and the pangs of doubt had begun to arise within. Would he show? This was a fools errand I told myself. What the devil was I doing? There was no way he would show. Why would he?

And yet...

For reasons I just cannot comprehend I somehow know that he will be here tonight. Then, as if on cue I look up and there he is sitting at a table close to the entrance.

ONE HOUR: TOTAL SURRENDER

Curious, I had not seen him enter. He glances at his watch, then orders a drink. A little later the doors open to allow the entrance of a tall and very striking red head with long flowing ringlet hair, she stops for a moment looks about, spots Nathaniel, then giving a big smile waves, then heads over to him. He stands up hugs her then kisses her forehead, they sit, Nathaniel orders more drinks and they remain talking for some time.

Raising my Iphone I zoom in on the two of them clicking a few shots. Examining the photos the red head is I concede exceptionally beautiful with pale skin and deep emerald green eyes. I can't help but feel a strong pang of jealousy at her. Over an hour later the two finish their drinks then leave the bar. As they exit through the doors I check my watch it reads 11.40 pm, then follow discretely behind observe them getting into a cab. As it pulls away I flag down another cab and get in. 'Follow that cab!' I order.

The driver turns and glares at me 'You having me on lady, they only say that in the movies.'

I feel myself wince for a second. 'If you want to earn some good money, follow that cab.'

The driver regards me for a moment, then shrugs. 'Sure lady, you got it.' With that the cab heads off. 'So what's the story lady? That ye husband or something?'

'You got it in one,' I say giving a stern reply. 'The cheating bastard's having an affair with his secretary and I intend to catch them in the act.'

'Alright! Let's go get em. This is better than the movies.' The driver exclaims

The cab eases along just keeping Bill's cab in sight, I figure it's heading for Bill's place we seemed to be heading to southern part of town. Eventually it pulls up outside the large house, Nathaniel and the red head exit the cab. 'Drive past and pull up on the corner I instruct, the cab driver nods then stops as instructed. 'That's 10.20.' He informs me as I exit the cab.

'Thanks, I didn't get your name?'

'Louie,' the driver replies with a grin.

'Thanks Louie,' I say handing him 50. 'I really appreciate your help. And you're right, it ain't like the movies.' As the cab pulls away I make my way slowly along the badly lit street, just in time to see Nathaniel and the redhead enter his house. Glancing at my watch it indicates it was just past midnight, then I make my way down a side alley that takes me around the rear of the house and upon a gate to the back yard, trying the catch, at first it feels stiff, placing my weight against it, it starts to give, a quick shove with my hip, there is a loud crack and the wooden gate opens allowing me to slip inside.

CHAPTER 7

My eyes slowly adjust to the dark, the semi moonlight aids me to see just enough to move safely through the yard as I push my way through some bushes towards the back of the house. The gravel crunches a little too loudly under my shoes, I freeze, I can just make out a small muddy pathway to my left, cautiously I move on to it, taking a few steps past another bush, then, curse as my foot steps in something, a puddle of some sort, the cold water sops over my shoe. I'm already regretting this venture, steeling myself I force myself on wards. Lights come on in various rooms inside the house, then go out except for one room on the ground floor. Crouching for a moment in the bushes, I take a handkerchief from my coat pocket and wipe the mud from the top of my foot and base of my ankle, I should have worn more sensible shoes. Then carefully I make my way forward towards the lights emanating from the two French doors. They are open slightly and draped inside with the long thick velvet like curtains that are not fully pulled together. Through the crack between them I can see directly inside into the large hall.

The redhead stands in the middle of the room her manacled wrists are attached to chains secured above her head the the large metal hook in the ceiling. Her sensuous mouth has a large red ball gag in it secured in place by a black leather strap. Her long legs are held wide apart by chains connected to leather straps around her ankles, the chains are linked to two metal rings in the floor. The redhead tugs futilely at the chains above her head, then tests the straps around her ankles she is held fast. Shaking her head she makes protest noises through the gag that emit as muffled whimpers, slivers of drool run down the sides of her mouth.

The outfit she is wearing is without doubt the kinkiest I've ever seen. Black boots that came up to her knees with very high heels, tight, shiny black latex crotchless pants showcasing her shaven sex clung to her legs and hips like a second skin. A tight shiny black latex bra with low cleavage, that show cases her ample assets that heave as I watch fixated. Her stomach is toned, and congruent with the rest of her athletic body and to cap it all, she had long black velvet gloves on that come all the way up her arms just past her elbows.

I am absolutely mesmerised by the redhead's struggles and helplessness. She is totally in Nathaniel's power, something I recall from my own experience.

At that moment he enters the room wearing a simple shirt, flannel like pants and soft shoes. Standing in front of the red head for a moment, he begins by checking the manacles, wrist chains, ankle straps and chains and lastly, the gag. Satisfied he produces a handkerchief and gently dabs the drool from the sides of her mouth, before moving behind her and running his finger tips down either side of her bare ribs to her hips, the red head shivers as he does so, giving out a muffled gasp. I watched utterly fixated as Nathaniel begins to toy with the redhead, her flaming hair is worn up, Nathaniel immediately releases the red locks allowing them to cascade over her shoulders. He then grabs a handful of the loose flowing hair roughly yanking back her head causing the woman to give out a muffled yelp lightly and sensuously kisses her exposed neck whilst gently fondling one of her large breasts. The woman gives out muffled moans of pleasure as he touches her and is immediately punished by having her hair yanked back hard. Nathaniel waggles a finger at her admonishing her for making a sound. Straining to listen I caught one word: '*Silence*.'

She manages to bob her head a little in acknowledgement, despite her hair still in his tight grip, then she visibly forces herself to focus by closing her eyes as he once again begins the slow and fateful stimulation of her body.

One breast, then the other was gently squeezed and fondled, her nipples stroked, then gently flicked through the dark thin latex, her breathing becomes deeper as she desperately tries to retain some form of control. His touch is that of an expert, gentle and loving at times, rougher at others. He once again starts with light kisses to her neck and shoulders, then nibbles at her ears, whispering things to her that are clearly having an effect. I catch sight of a smug smile as he stands behind her cupping her breasts his finger tips brushing her now rigid nipples causing her to jerk.

Pausing for a moment he reaches to a nearby table picked up a small paddle with a long narrow handle, turning it flat he begins to slowly pat her exposed sex with a resounding Pap, Pap, Pap. The impacts causes the red head to whimper and rock back and forth. Pap, Pap, Pap. More whimpers, the redhead throws her head backwards trying to maintain some semblance of control. Then using his index finger and thumb he parts her outer lips exposing her inner lips and clitoris. Pap, Pap, Pap, This time the redhead's eyes widen as she jerks from the impacts. Then his index finger began stroking her clitoris slow, gentle, brushing it, then adding a little pressure, the red head takes in a deep audible breath through her nostrils as he did so.

All the while this takes place I kneel quietly observing, experiencing conflicting emotions of repulsion at the degrading treatment being met out on the redhead. Whilst at the same time, becoming mesmerised and intensely aroused by the incredibly kinky spectacle before me. What the hell was I doing here? I have lost all sense of my purpose. I'm now perving on Nathaniel and his kinky girl friend?

What had he done to me? And what was I becoming?

The questions vanish in a moment as I continue fixated to watch them, my hand moves slowly beneath my skirt, finger tips brush aside the now damp material of my panties, coming into contact with the furrow of my wet sex. I find myself with a deep yearning to be in the place of the redhead, a yearning that screams within me. "Oh, to be Nathaniel's captive and sex toy, once again and be tortured so exquisitely."

Opening my eyes I watch breathlessly as Nathaniel abruptly stops and moves away from the redhead, her eyes open with a flash of anger and frustration as he just stands watching her silently denying her the pleasure and release she so craves. Then he turns to examine a number of implements on the nearby table, as he does so the red head glances up and our eyes meet.

I freeze, as she spots me. Our eyes lock I am rooted to the spot. In that instant something strange takes place. My immediate instinct is to run, dash back to the back gate and get the hell out. But I can't move. I can't move at all. My mind comes to complete stop. Any thoughts of running, getting the hell out — hang frozen in mid air as her emerald green eyes suddenly blaze with an incredible intensity. A wave of nausea sweeps over me with an over whelming force, my vision blurs I feel as though I might pass out as the redhead jumps in and out of focus followed by a loud drumming in my mind, Badoom, Badoom, Badoom the sound grew louder and louder, almost deafening. Followed by a rushing wind like sound in my ears. A violent jerk forward and sudden acceleration I am dragged towards her. Then, a with a sudden jolt my eyes open.

For a moment I'm totally disorientated, everything around me is a blur, as it slowly settles. I'm standing up. I am indeed standing up, my arms are above my head,confusion and panic sweeps through me my wrists are secured above me looking up, they are manacled chained above my head. I'm wearing arm length black velvet gloves, long ringlets of red hair lay down my shoulders.

What...?

My mouth, my mouth is stuffed with something large, tasting of rubber, drool runs down my chin...Desperately I glance about the room I now find myself...In the middle of the room, Nathaniel has his back to me stooping over a table looking at various items placing a paddle down he picks up another but slightly smaller one then turns to face me. My whole body is on fire, my nipples are hard and erect aching with an exquisite pain. Below I feel sexual heat and wetness...I glance up to the French doors across the room, there crouching outside the doors peering in I can just make out...

Me!

CHAPTER 8

It is Me. Or the exact image of me that watches intently as Nathaniel advances I can do nothing but stare at him, and the image of me as he gently parts the lips of my sex using his middle finger to brush my clit forcing me to jerk in the chains, letting out a muffled moan of pleasure through the gag. Then he starts a firm Pap, Pap, Pap with the paddle upon my exposed sex. I tense as the paddle impacts letting out a muffled whimper. Then another Pap, and another Pap, followed by a steady over and over, the effect is incredible. I feel myself tense as something within begins to take form. Sensing my predicament Nathaniel ceases for a brief moment, grabs my hair with a painful jerk. *'I told you. Don't you dare come until, I give you permission. Understand?'* He hisses into my ear before continuing. I manage to bob my head in acknowledgement.

Then he begins again. Only this time a finger brushes lightly over my clit. He is relentless, I try to focus, to block out the intense stimulation that is now threatening to overwhelm me.

Pap, Pap,Pap...I let out a muffled cry through the gag. Nathaniel stops, remains silent for a moment then turns the paddle dipping the handle into my pussy twirling it round and round as it rubs inside, stimulating my G-spot. At the same time he slips a nipple out of the latex bra and starts to slowly squeeze it between forefinger and thumb, before rolling it.

ONE HOUR: TOTAL SURRENDER

My head jerks, I start to snort loudly then bite down hard on the rubber ball gag trying desperately to maintain some form of control, fighting to keep back any sound my body starts to jerk as I fight desperately to maintain some form of control, but I know it is futile. Nathaniel continues for sometime before finally inserting his fingers into my slit then removes them they glistened, dripping with my juices.

He grabs me by her hair with a hard yank showing me his fingers. Shaking his head, there is a twinkle of fun in his eyes. He moves over to the far wall before reaching for something in the corner, it is a little over 30 centimetres in length, black in colour and cordless with a large black head. Switching it on, it emits a low buzzing noise something that I am intimately familiar with. Nathaniel begins to gently press it between my legs my wet hot furrow becoming instantly stimulated. Nathaniel then whispers in my ear, I'm ordered not to climax, I must not under any circumstances until — he gives permission. '*Obey me you wanton slut.*' He whispers. Then continues to work upon me, stroking the head of the device back and forth over my exposed sex. Gently, slowly, upping it making me fight to maintain control.

I must not...

My head shoots up towards the French windows the image of me looks on with a deep satisfied smile, sadistically enjoying my torture, the image of me holds up her hand, fingers glistening then she begins to slowly brush them across her lips, her eyes squint and a grin of satisfaction crosses her face as she slowly licks and sucks her finger tips. I'm being tortured, no matter how I try it is impossible to hold back the exquisite stimulation of the Hitachi in Nathaniel's expert hands is just too much and eventually...

There is a sudden jolt of electric through my body, becoming instantly rigid, then my entire body convulses, I tug wildly and involuntarily at the unyielding chains above my head and ankles that hold me fast. Crying out through the gag in a long muffled mind fucking scream before going completely limp. I dangle like a floppy doll from the chains, all energy having been sapped from me like a sponge my breathing is deep and furious. I feel a hand grab my hair tugging it up the blurry vision of Nathaniel is before me.

'I did not give you permission — Bitch.' He whispers with a snarl. I can only manage to bob my head a little in agreement. My head drops back limply as he releases my hair.

Forcing myself to look up is almost impossible, I just manage to once again locking eyes with the image of me.

Her eyes glow with an intense green, once again a wave of nausea sweeps over me, my vision blurs the image of me jumps in and out of focus followed by the loud drumming in my mind, that I had experienced before, Badoom, Badoom, Badoom it grows louder and louder, I'm certain I hear an amused giggling as a loud rushing wind sounds in my ears, followed by a violent jerk, sudden acceleration and I am propelled at speed towards the image of me.

Then — with a sudden jolt my eyes open.

I am outside. Above me the moon and stars shine brightly. I am laying on my back and try to prop myself up on an elbow but slump back with a thud, hitting my head. I have absolutely no strength. How long I lay there I really don't know, perhaps ten or fifteen minutes, I started to shiver, it was getting pretty chilly. Eventually I slowly manage to stand with quite some effort, supporting myself against the wall my legs are like rubber, staggering I sort my clothing. What the hell had just happened to me?

When I was finally able to force myself to walk, I glance at my watch it reads 1.40 am, then look inside through the French doors Nathaniel and the redhead are nowhere to be seen. Reaching to a handle I pull one of the doors open, then enter the room. The chains dangle from the hook in the ceiling, the ball gag hangs from a hook on the wall. The large metal rings that kept the red head's legs spread open lay flat on the floor. On a small table laid out are a number of implements, varying types of whips as well as the paddles, I'd seen used on the redhead and me earlier.

Had it truly been me? I wonder, as I replay the whole scene, it had truly been as if I was the read head. My mind races to make sense of it but nothing explains what I had experienced. Examining the paddles I notice the the smallest, the handle still glistened with juices. Other gags hang on the wall black leather types that cover over the mouth with hard large rubber cocks poking up from the middle that would go in the woman's mouth before being secured. Examining these items I am once more both strangely repelled and entranced by them.

At that moment I sense movement to my left turning, I spin around and came face to face with the red head. She smiles, then everything around me starts fade in and out, the room begins to revolve, slowly at first then faster, and faster my stomach lurches in a way one experiences on a roller coaster that is the last sensation I recall as everything fades in blackness.

CHAPTER 9

I awaken painfully slowly, it is an effort to force myself through the wooziness, it's like wading through thick treacle each step a major effort until... Finally, I break free to intense brightness that forces me to close my eyes from the glare, it slowly recedes to be replaced by a wave of nausea and dizziness as the ceiling spins with incredible speed above me. Mercifully, the spinning comes to a stop with a gut wrenching jolt. Disorientated a rising panic begins to take hold, taking slow deep breaths I just manage to keep the panic in check. I am laid out on a soft surface. A slight cold draught from my left causes me shiver, followed by the realisation that I am completely naked. Raising my head confirms this and I'm met with a wave of dizziness for my trouble, with a moan my head flumps back onto the soft support of a pillow. With some effort I manage to force myself to roll onto my right side, overcoming the feelings of nausea and dizziness that still linger. I'm laying in the middle of a large wooden four poster bed in an otherwise bare room, one not unlike the one I watched Bill and the redhead in. There is no other furniture or fittings, save for a pair long dark velvet curtains to my left covering a window, they billow a little from the cool breeze, to my right there is a door.

ONE HOUR: TOTAL SURRENDER

At that moment I hear the sound of approaching footsteps I make out a shadow of movement just under the base of the door, there is a clicking like a key in a lock, rolling back I close my eyes pretending to still be unconscious. The door opens, I sense someone entering, perhaps more than one, more footsteps, that grow closer.

'So, nosey bitch did you enjoy watching us.' Comes a female voice, clearly the redhead with undisguised contempt. 'And you can stop pretending I know you're awake.'

Opening my eyes I find myself staring into the scowling face of the redhead. Seeing her close up she is now wearing a just a white bath robe. Her red ringlet hair is loose and flowing. Up close she is a stunning woman her deep emerald green eyes seem to blaze with a strange sexual aura that causes my nipples respond instantly, aching with need. As if conscious of this her eyes glance down for a moment to my breasts then back up I catch the flicker of a satisfied smile. She sits on the bed next to me and starts to gently stroke my hair. '*I have to confess snoop,*' she whispers. '*Knowing you were watching earlier made me soooo wet. More so than what he was doing to me.*' She purrs continuing to stroke. '*Did you get off on it too? Did you get off watching what he was doing to me?*'

She bends closer her mouth barely inches from my ear, her warm breath makes me shiver, my nipples ache in unison. '*I know you did. You so wanted to be in my place didn't you?*' Her whisper is breathless, turning to face her I glare at her unable to respond.

She giggles mischievously, '*How did it feel— taking my place for those exquisite moments?*' She bends forward we are almost nose to nose, her eyes blaze with a green fury. '*Couldn't help yourself though,could you? It's impossible to resist when he plays with you. I should know — I've been trying to do so now for... Well Forever!'* She giggles once more. *'If I can't resist him, what chance does a pathetic, dirty snooping mortal bitch like you have?'*

I am totally unable to respond my mind replaying the whole experience once again I see the image of me... Had it been an image?

'You really don't get it do you?' She shakes her head then begins to laugh. *'You mortals just do not comprehend what is possible. It was delicious, truly delicious. I got to watch you being used by him, it was so good that I fingered myself — or should that be you?* She shrugs. *In any case It brought me to mind fucking climax. So I thank you for the spectacle.'*

'What... What is going on?' I manage to speak, my voice somewhat croaky. 'Why are you doing this to me...' The red head places a gentle finger to my lips with a 'Shhhhh.' Then stands back from the bed towering over me her eyes glide over my body. At the same time she reaches down to the belt around her robe unfastens it then, with a slow deliberateness that mesmerises me she slips the robe back over her shoulders letting it slide gently down her arms to reveal her in her nakedness.

Standing at over 6 feet tall she is an imposing looking woman with a toned athletic body, I hear myself take a deep breath at her incredible form. Her skin is pale almost a milky white a stark contrast to her fiery red hair. In the light the freckles on her face, shoulders and around her firm large breasts are visible, facing me her magnificent naked Amazonian body almost glows.

'Like what you see Blondie?' She whispers with a sinister smile. Her eyes wash over me with an intensity of a predator about to devour its prey. *'Now lets see what we have here.'* With

that the red head lays out next to me, then pauses momentarily her eyes widen drinking in my naked body and heaving breasts. *'I see why Nathaniel fell for you so hard, he has such exquisite taste. But You know, it's not just men who appreciate a nice pair of tits and long legs,'* she giggles again as her finger gently circles the hard point of my nipple. *'And you—come very well equipped. I bet you turn heads all the time male—and female.'* Her emerald eyes glow with a soft luminescence, as her fingers gently stroke my shoulder, I shiver, then she leans forward her lips lightly brush mine, warm breath tickles my cheek, then our lips meet in slow motion, gentle, sensuous. My heart pounds like a jack hammer in my chest as I feel her hand cup my left breast squeezing it softly, her thumb lightly brushing the nipple causes me to gasp. Then she moves to my neck her moist lips brushing down wards, then kissing lightly upwards. Taking a deep breath I raise my head offering myself to her. I am totally unable to resist as her thumb now starts to make circles around my nipple causing it to become rigid. As if on cue she moves from my neck down to the waiting nipple lightly kissing it. Then takes it in her mouth and begins to gently suck it before swirling her tongue around it. Pulling away for a moment she gazes upon me as my breasts heave. Her eyes blaze with a deep green glow that robs me of any will. I can only manage a moan as she pushes me back without resisting I go with it as she guides me backwards onto the pillow. As my head lands upon the soft welcoming embrace of the pillow, she moves to the other nipple her mouth working its magic upon it. Arching my back I groan in pleasure my right hand reaches out to stroke her long red mane as she moves from the nipple down my abdomen, the tip of her tongue lightly stabs my belly button causing me to giggle and gasp at the pleasure she is giving me.

'*That's a good girl just let go,*' she whispers. *Just surrender—to Biata.*' Her voice echoes softly over and over within my mind. '*Surrr— render— to Biata. Totally, Surrr— render— to Biata.*'

Her head hovers between my legs, our eyes meet for a brief moment, opening my legs wider I raise my hips inviting her in. Her lips lightly kissing my inner thighs, gentle, loving then her tongue traces the line of my sex, her fingers lightly parted the outer lips spreading me open as her tongue slides along the furrow between.

It was beyond words I was being taken by a woman and I was loving every second of of it. Her tongue swirls around my clit, gently at first, causing me to gasp. James had always considered himself a master at going down upon me but what the redhead was doing to me made all that seem— trite. I gasp and moan surrendering to the total bliss. I sense her slide a finger into me with no resistance I'm surprised at just how wet I am. Her finger pushes deep within then twists and pumps in and out as her mouth continues to work in a slow rhythmic fashion upon my clit. The one finger becomes two or three, I can't be sure and it truly doesn't matter at this point. All I know is that I am in the grip of something I had never before experienced. Her mouth works its magic upon me, that tongue of hers...

Oh — my— God!

I feel the muscles of my abdomen and thighs start to jerk, my hips convulse up against her fingers and mouth as I start to moan, the sound catches in my throat as I breathe in deeply. Her tongue increases in speed now placing pressure upon my sensitive bud, whilst her fingers continue to pump within.

I've experienced orgasms.

But I've never experienced ORGASMS!

ONE HOUR: TOTAL SURRENDER

I twist, buck then let out a scream as my entire being explodes. Then collapse limp breathing deeply for a few minutes then there is movement on the bed. I open my eyes everything around me is a post orgasmic haze.

Something brushes against my hips then ribs as she slid over my breasts, followed by pressure on my upper chest she kneels astride me. *'I hope you were paying attention as it's your turn now. Make me come Justine. Make—me—come.'* Bearing down on me her soft moist sex presses down against my mouth, my tongue pushed out to lick her glistening slit. Excitement overtakes me as I began to lick and suck she begins grind herself against my mouth almost suffocating me for a moment. Overcome by the intense arousal I was experiencing, it didn't matter, nothing mattered except focusing upon her — I must satisfy Biata. That is her name. It was my purpose. My only purpose as her voice rebounded and echoed inside my mind: *'Make me come Justine. Make—me—come. Make me come Justine. Make—me—come.'* For a brief moment a realisation hits me. She'd called me by my name, not, Blondie, snoop, slut or anything derogatory.

Biata bears down onto me, her breathing becoming more ragged, gasping as she grinds her sex into my face as I continue to lick faster, my tongue swirled around her clit, then I suck, she starts to shudder then make gurgling noises followed by crying out. Her head flies back her rd locks float and sway in slow motion, her hands press down hard on the bed. She remained still for a few minutes riding out the after shocks, then gently dismounted and lay down beside me with a satisfied smile, we kiss gently, sensuously then cuddle together relishing our connection in the blissful afterglow, before falling into an exhausted sleep.

CHAPTER 10

I awaken to the feeling of Biata rolling away from me she climbs effortlessly off the bed then puts her robe back on and fastens the belt. Pulling the sheet from the bed I wrap it around me the draught from the window makes me shiver, before I can can say anything she looks up her green eyes begin to glow *'I know you have a thousand questions just wanting to be answered.'* Her voice is in my head. *'You want to know why we brought you here?'*

'You. You brought me here?'

'Yes Justine, we brought you here. You've been experiencing major sexual urges. Insatiable sexual cravings. Acting like a total slut?' I bristle for a moment as Biata steps in front me only inches away. My breath catches in my throat, she is so imposing and incredibly beautiful her emerald green eyes blaze in a bright hypnotic florescence. *'It's like you are a completely different person isn't it?'* I can only nod in agreement totally unable to speak *'Especially after the way you seduced your poor unsuspecting P.A. the other nigh. Throwing yourself so aggressively at him. You really are quite the predator Justine, for a mortal that is.'*

'How…How did you…' I am literally lost for words

Biata giggles then circles me like a lioness her cleavage heaving just under the loosely open robe. I can do nothing but follow her as I am captive to the mesmerising gaze of her eyes.

ONE HOUR: TOTAL SURRENDER

'*It is really very simple,*' Biata begins. '*When Nathaniel took you as his lover he violated our most sacred rule. Never become intimate with a mortal. We are only permitted to guide,*' Biata continues. '*But Never. Never to become intimate.*'

My mind races at what she is telling me, then something within strikes a chord as I respond, 'Why, because we mortals are...So fragile?' At this Biata raises an eyebrow.

'*Something like that. What you are experiencing are the after affects of your love making with Nathaniel. Regular sexual encounters with us have been known to drive some mortals crazy, others. Others, sadly to self destruction. The effects would have receded, in time. Only, now it will take considerably longer, owing to...*' Biata pauses for a moment.

'Owing to you taking me last night.' I reply. Biata just gives me a wink then heads to the door and opens it to reveal Nathaniel in the doorway, my heart races at sight of him.

'*Hello Justine, welcome back to my realm.*'

His soft voice is inside my head, I glance to Biata then then to him, I feel my blood boil. 'If you are both through with the magic tricks I want to know what the hell is going on.'

'*Closure Justine.*' Nathaniel replies taking a step towards me. '*What Biata told you is completely true. I've been watching you all your life, watch you develop and achieve. The pride I felt in you as you did so, well I just don't have the words. Then when James left, you looked so sad and I wanted to comfort you. So I came to aid you but as we talked I allowed my desires to take control of me.*'

'But it was more than just desire for Justine wasn't it Nathaniel?' Biata cuts in.

He merely nods remaining silent then steps forward places a finger on my forehead in a second the fuzziness in my head clears. I can remember. I can remember everything...

I'm laying on the sofa in his home, he kneels next to me gently stroking my face. I'm utterly exhausted following our love making but feel amazing. 'Nathaniel. What are you?' I ask.

Then his voice is in my mind *'I told you in the bar. And now, I have shown my true form to you.'* He pauses for a moment. *'I'm only permitted to guide you through your crisis... Not...*

'Seduce and fuck me senseless?' I reply running my hand gently through his soft hair.

He smiles.*'Crudely put, but accurate.* His voice is curiously in my mind his kiss soft and gentle as he gently bites my lower lip. *'Did I hurt you?'* His voice is soft sounds inside my mind. Pulling I shake my head. His face one of great concern. *'I'm so relieved. You mortals are so fragile. I could have seriously hurt you.'*

'Well you were rather, shall we say, Primal.' I say examining the bruises on my arms, legs and shoulder. 'Somewhat Frantic.' I recall the sensations from earlier as he took me. Nathaniel on top of me, then behind as he took me on all fours. Then — I am riding him. My arms are now bound behind my back, the stocking gag is dripping wet with saliva as I bite down on it. As Nathaniel works his magic on me, my need for him is insatiable. I'm impaled my internal muscles gripping his iron cock, I can feel he is almost ready to come.

Then, I am standing against the wall the gag is removed from my mouth the wet stocking dangles loosely around my neck specks of saliva drip onto my breasts. His Wings flap gently then seem to fold back as he lifted one of my legs to his waist. Our eyes met, no words were necessary my arms are now around his strong neck, then he is inside me my legs wrap around his waist as he fucked me against the wall. Thud. Thud. Thud.

'Then there was the incredibly kinky, tying me up, gagging me keeping me as your sexual play thing. I didn't know what to make of it at first, it was almost as if you knew my darkest secrets.'

He smiles knowingly *'I could have so easily have seriously hurt you Justine and... I couldn't bare it that I had.'* He turns away for a moment.

'What is it Nathaniel?' I ask reaching out.

'I love you Justine. That is what is wrong. I love you and have done so for a long time. You are such an incredible woman. Strong, beautiful, successful...'

'But pretty shitty at relationships.' I chuckle.

'Well no one's perfect.' Nathaniel grins. *'You have no concept of the existence I have Justine as an eternal being, not subject to injury, disease and ageing that you as a mortal must contend with. In comparison, your existence is as brief to me as that of— a butterfly. That is the curse of being eternal, to have to watch that which you love eventually die. That's why I brought you to my realm so we could be together.'*

In that moment I understood. We made love again, but much slower, gentle. I had never experienced such tenderness, it was truly overwhelming. Afterwards as we lay on the sofa his eyes spoke to me I understood, simply nodded, he takes my hand and then something happens, the room spins violently I feel his hand hold me firm then the spinning room stops with an almost sickening lurch. Nathaniel helps me up and I get dressed my actions almost autonomous his soft voice seemingly inside my mind giving me commands, my head bobs in confirmation. He kisses me, strokes my hair then leads me gently through the house to the front door. One last kiss, then I step outside and walk down the path onto the street, the cold wind is biting as I head towards the waiting cab yet, I barely notice. Opening the cab door, I climb in give the driver my address then as the cab pulls away I slowly nod off in the back to the gentle rocking of the car.

Opening my eyes Nathaniel and Biata stand quietly. everything now makes complete sense. The enhanced sex drives, the visions, the loss of time. I turn to Biata, before I can utter a word.

'I was curious,' she begins as if reading my mind. 'And as I said to you earlier, quite jealous that he would be so strongly attracted to a mortal. I confess, I held you in such contempt. But then, I saw your qualities, your strength of spirit, you have incredible sexual drives. I discovered those when we switched places. I've never encountered a mortal quite like you, it was confusing at first and incredibly refreshing. You have no idea what an incredible gift that is. I knew that like Nathaniel I had to have you.'

'Justine,' Nathaniel cuts in. 'You should know Biata is my...'

'Your what exactly?' The red head stands tall with folded arms.

ONE HOUR: TOTAL SURRENDER

'Biata, is...' Nathaniel glances at me then eyes the red head with a loving smile. 'Is many things to me, as you saw earlier she is my sexual play thing, I do so love indulging my darker side with you Biata.' His eyes glaze over as he becomes momentarily distant, lost in some day dream. 'She's also my fantasy woman, fuck toy, Lover, and — what, a lover! But above all. Biata is my long time companion and — dare I say Soul mate.'

'Oh Nathaniel.' Biata purrs. 'But now, so is Justine.'

'*Yes my love, she is indeed.* Nathaniel smiles. *'It is time for you to go now Justine.'* His voice is inside my head.

'*But first a parting gift.'* Comes Biata's voice. '*For now anyway.'* She gives me a knowing wink. At this Nathaniel slowly removes his shirt and pants, Biata once again disrobes in a moment they are totally naked before me. I watch my mouth agape as both Nathaniel and Biata begin to glow with a bright white glow. Then a pair of large white feathery wings begin to slowly sprout from the tops of his muscled shoulders opening wide. Nathaniel stands before me in a ball of bright light, with wings protruding out beautiful white feathers with burnt black tips running along the top and side edges. The wings are huge reaching down almost to Bills ankles. Biata also sprouts wings that are pure white, they too almost reach down to her ankles. As I stare at the visions before me my mind seems to slow and become calm as if with an unspoken comprehension. Nathaniel and Biata move slowly towards me, Biata gently removes the sheet from me then guides me onto the bed. Curiously I don't register any weight as they climb on to the bed either side of me, their wings gently flap creating a cool breeze. Biata's mouth meets mine, gentle and sensuous, caressing my cheek, she kisses me softly, nibbling my lower lip. My breath catches then resumes hard and fast with desire. Her hands begin to explore my body. In a moment I am enveloped by a reassuring softness and warmth followed by the most incredible sensations. Her green eyes blaze, pupils dilated and wanton. Pulling away she whispers to me to get on all fours. What can I do? I had to comply. Raising my head Biata offers her sex to me I began to gently kiss and lick just as Nathaniel stands behind, his hands brush my buttocks, I can hear his his breathing deep and rapid, I feel his hard cock rubbing against my backside as I am focused upon Biata. When he impales me... It is all I can do not to let out a scream of total ecstasy as my body reacts to him. He stays still for sometime allowing me to experience him deep within me then begins to thrust, slow and gentle at first, then they start to build becoming harder, fucking harder.

My last memory is feeling Biata begin to climax as my own was also building then everything around me starts to spin slowly then faster and faster fading into black.

CHAPTER 11

I awaken with a start to a sensation of moving, the side to side motion of being in a car momentarily disorientates me. My mind is a little foggy, my whole body resonates with a strange static like charge. The last thing I remember is being taken by Nathaniel and Biata. The thought causes an involuntary shiver and flush of wetness. Images race through my mind, vivid flashes of:

Nathaniel as he takes me deep from behind, as my mouth brings Biata to climax...

Then Biata has me lay back on the bed and secures my wrists above my head. Opening my legs she kneels and begins to pleasure me with her mouth, licking sucking, closing my eyes I hear myself gasp with each incredibly vivid and vibrant flash of memory. Being taken by her as I raise my hips to her wanting her to make me hers her large magnificent wings flap gently creating a soft cooling breeze...

I feel it within building from far below gathering speed roaring on wards sending me into a maelstrom of building orgasm as it begins rolling with increased momentum towards its zenith, more flashes, her mouth working its magic on my clit. My body is aflame. Oh my God. I feel myself coming as my whole body stiffens against the seat. Every fibre of me is literally going to combust.

And then—I go limp falling into the back seat of the cab chest heaving rapidly. Regaining my senses I realised that I was once more in the back of a cab.

At that very moment the cab comes to an abrupt halt halt. 'We're here lady.' The cab driver declares, glancing over at me

'Here?' I mumble looking around trying to make sense of the situation. 'Here? Where?'

The driver turns and giving me a quizzical look 'Where you asked to go, 475 Laycome. That'll be 14.75.'

'Where, I...' I stopped recognising we were outside my house, feeling a surge of De Ja Vu. 'Yes, yes of course, I'm so sorry,' I mumble sounding not very convincing. 'It's been a really long day.' I glance at my watch it reads 3.05 am. No, that couldn't be right. Could it? Then glance at the drivers dashboard it read. 3.06 am.

The driver regards me silently for a moment, 'Are you sure you're okay miss?'

'What? Yes, thank you,' I said handing him a twenty, 'keep the change.'

'Sure he replies smiling.'

My legs barely support me as I exit the cab then stagger like a drunk towards my door. Once inside I stagger into my lounge and flump out in a chair. More visions shoot through my mind as:

Nathaniel and Biata make love to me. I kneel as Biata is behind me fondling one of my sensitive breasts whilst her fingers are inside my wet slit fucking me. At the same time I take Nathaniel's erect cock in my mouth.

ONE HOUR: TOTAL SURRENDER

The vision and sensation fades leaving me limp and exhausted in the chair. I manage to stagger up the stairs to my bedroom then take a long shower, before I crash out on my bed.

Later that morning I get up at about 10 am change into some loose clothing then decide to make a few calls, starting with my parents.

'Hi Mom, Merry Christmas. How's dad?..'

Having caught up with family and friends I sit back in my chair sipping coffee, then the urge to make one more call hits me.

For a moment I hesitate, we hadn't really spoken since the Christmas party and...

What the hell I press the call button on my cell. 'Ryan. Hi, it's Justine...'

Some time later there is a knock at my door, I open it to find Ryan looking a little nervous or— is it excitement?

'Hi, Justine. You asked me to come over, said it was urgent.'

'Yes I did, come in.'

Ryan follows me inside. 'I hope I didn't disturb your Christmas plans Ryan.' I say pushing the door closed behind me with my butt.

'What? Eh, no, I didn't really have any, was just going to spend Christmas in my apartment...'

Our eyes lock for a second. '*Say my name.*' I whisper. Moving slowly towards him.

'*Justine.*' Comes a breathless reply

'*Say it again.*' I order.

'*Justine.*' He gasps as our mouths meet hungrily.

'*It's not appropriate for a P.A. to act like this.*' I whisper in his ear. '*But it is — for a lover.*

Later I slip out of bed, Ryan is still sleeping. I make my way down stairs into the kitchen, pour a cold drink from the refrigerator then glance into the lounge where our clothes lay strewn across the floor. A rush of warmth surges through me at the memory of the intensity of our love making my wanton need for Ryan, what had Nathaniel said? It would pass in time. Truth to tell I hope it never does. At this thought, something directs me to reach into my coat pocket that is hung over the chair. I fumble about inside then touch something soft. My hand comes out holding two feathers, a deep white one and one white with black tips. '*Merry Fucking Christmas Justine.*' I whisper feeling an intense warmth within.

Don't miss out!

Visit the website below and you can sign up to receive emails whenever Alexis Ryder publishes a new book. There's no charge and no obligation.

https://books2read.com/r/B-A-CFTJ-XXBDB

BOOKS 2 READ

Connecting independent readers to independent writers.